FAR OUT
FAIRY TALES

STONE ARCH BOOKS
a capstone imprint

DOC

TRASH TALK

THE SEVEN ROBOTS

Far Out Fairy Tales is published by
Stone Arch Books
A Capstone Imprint
1710 Roe Crest Drive, North Mankato,
Minnesota 56003
www.capstonepub.com

Cataloging-in-Publication Data is
available at the Library of Congress
website.
Hardcover ISBN: 978-1-4342-9648-1
Paperback ISBN: 978-1-4342-9652-8

Summary: On a distant planet called
Techworld, a little girl named Snow
White is created by the planet's
smartest minds to be the perfect
scientist, Snow immediately shows a
knack for working with electronics.
The Queen Regent, fearing for her
crown, exiles Snow White so she
cannot grow up and take the queen's
place as the most intelligent person on
the planet.

Lettering by Jaymes Reed.

Designer: Bob Lentz
Editor: Sean Tulien
Managing Editor: Donald Lemke
Creative Director: Heather Kindseth
Editorial Director: Michael Dahl
Publisher: Ashley C. Andersen Zantop

Printed in the United States of
America in North Mankato, Minnesot
052015   008968R

SNOW WHITE

AND THE

SEVEN ROBOTS

A GRAPHIC NOVEL

BY LOUISE SIMONSON
ILLUSTRATED BY JIMENA SÁNCHEZ

Come on in and make yourself at home!

And yes, we have extra fuel.

I can pay, of course. And I offer this as an extra thank you for your kindness.

Chocolate? I haven't tasted it in *ages!*

NOM!

We gave Snow White a ruler's gifts, but Queen Regent tried to make her monstrous!

She's no monster. She's the smartest human *ever*. Look how she fixed me!

Yes! She is kind. She helped us *all!*

As soon as the ship landed...

The queen drove Snow White into exile. She tried to kill her...

...but now Snow has returned!

All Hail *Queen Snow White!!*

ALL ABOUT THE ORIGINAL TALE!

The story of Snow White was first published by the Brothers Grimm in 1812. This fairy tale tells the story of a queen who wishes for a daughter with skin as white as snow, lips as red as blood, and jet-black hair. She gets her wish, but tragically dies during childbirth.

Snow White's father then marries a beautiful but selfish woman. Each day, the new queen asks a magic mirror who the most beautiful woman alive is. And each day, the mirror says it's the queen--until one day the mirror names Snow White instead.

The queen decides to have Snow killed. She orders a huntsman to murder her, but he can't make himself do the deed so he abandons her in the forest instead. Snow comes across a tiny cottage with seven small beds. As it turns out, seven dwarves live there, and they let her stay with them in exchange for keeping their home tidy and making their meals.

Soon after, the magic mirror tells the queen where Snow is hiding. The queen arrives disguised as a farmer's wife and offers Snow a poisoned apple, which puts Snow into a permanent state of sleep. When the dwarves return from work, they think Snow is dead, so they place her in a glass coffin.

One day, a prince comes along and is struck by Snow White's beauty. The dwarves let the prince take the coffin, presumably so she can have a proper burial. As the dwarves carry the coffin away, they trip and drop it. The bump dislodges the chunk of apple that was caught in Snow's throat, and she awakens! (In some versions of the tale, it's the prince's kiss that wakes Snow White from her endless sleep.) Either way, Snow falls in love with the prince at first sight. They marry, live happily ever after, and the evil queen is punished for her misdeeds.

In this far out version of the fairy tale, it's Snow White's inner beauty and intelligence that the queen fears. Check out this book's other twists to the timeless tale...

A **FAR OUT** GUIDE TO SNOW WHITE'S TALE TWISTS!

The all-knowing magic mirror is replaced by an all-seeing space satellite!

Dwarves helped the original Snow White. In this tale, robots come to her aid!

Instead of a poisoned apple putting Snow to sleep, poisoned chocolate is the culprit.

This cryo-tank preserves Snow White instead of the glass coffin in the original tale.

1

Why does Doc throw Snow White's backpack in the mud? How do you know?

2

The robots have to put Snow White in a cryo-coffin, or suspended animation, to keep her safe until they can cure her. How do you think this cryo-tank works? How might it prevent her from dying? Explain your answer.

3

KISS.

What do you think caused Snow White to wake up? Why?

4

A moral is a lesson that a story teaches. What do you think the moral of this story is? Why?

5

What big role did this little robot play in the story? How did he end up saving Snow White? Why do you think he helped?

AUTHOR

Louise Simonson writes about monsters, science fiction and fantasy characters, and superheroes. She wrote the award-winning Power Pack series, several best-selling X-Men titles, Web of Spider-man for Marvel Comics, and Superman: Man of Steel and Steel for DC Comics. She has also written many books for kids. She is married to comic artist and writer Walter Simonson and lives in the suburbs of New York City.

ILLUSTRATOR

Jimena Sánchez was born in Mexico City, Mexico, in 1980. She studied illustration in the Escuela Nacional de Artes Plásticas (National School of Arts) and has since worked and lived in the United States as well as Spain. Jimena now lives in Mexico City again, working as an illustrator and comic book artist. Her art has appeared in many children's books and magazines.